MORE ADVENTURES OF THE SUPERKIDS

LIBRARY

Flat Tire

Illustrated by

Susan Jaekel

ROWLAND READING FOUNDATION

MADISON, WISCONSIN

Units 1-3
Flat Tire

y
- by
- good-by
- sky
- ⭐ anyone
- chilly
- clunkety
- every

everybody
fluffy
funny
happy
hungry
silly
suddenly

☆ anyway
day
playing
say
way

-ier
chillier
hungrier

-iest
laziest

Trickers
broken
cozy
crazy
even
lazy
open
over
roly-poly
shady

couldn't   weren't   wouldn't

down   too   work   first   their
now   always   because   been

firefighters   should

⭐ When a word ends in *y* and has at least one other vowel, the *y* stands for the long *e* sound.

☆ When a word has two vowels together, the first is usually long and the second is silent.

On the way home from Happy Land,
the Superkids were sleeping on the cozy bus.
Sal held his new shocking-pink monster doll.
It was a prize from Happy Land. Sal liked
the doll because it was soft and roly-poly.

Suddenly, a big CLUNK, CLUNKETY, CLUNK
woke the Superkids.

Gus slammed on the brakes. "I am afraid
we have a flat tire," he said.

3

Doc got up. "Hot Rod," she said. "You have always been crazy about buses and trucks. I like to fix things. We can help Gus and Gert."

"I will help, too," said Sal.

"Oh, no thanks," said Doc. "We can handle it."

Sal saw that Ettabetta and Oswald were playing Tic-Tac-Toe. "You two are good at printing," Sal said to them. "You could make a big banner to say, 'Look out! Broken down bus!' "

"O.K.!" said Oswald and Ettabetta.

"Can I help?" asked Sal.

"Oh, no thanks," said Ettabetta. "We can handle it. Besides, we have only two pens."

Lily, Icky, and Toc had their silly hats on.

"You three could put on a show," said Sal.
"That would pass the time."

"Yes," said Tic. "Toc and I can teach you
funny songs to sing."

"Can the rest of us be in the show, too?" asked Sal.

"Oh, no thanks," said Tic. "We can handle it. Besides, if we were all in the show, there wouldn't be anyone to clap!"

"I am too chilly and hungry to sing anyway," said Cass. "I am chillier and hungrier every second!"

"There is a blanket on the bus," said Sal. "We could use it to make a tent. Gus has matches, so he can make a campfire."

"I like to put up tents," said Alf. "I will get the blanket."

"I will gather sticks," said Frits. "Then I will ask Gus to get the fire going."

"I will open a bag of fruit," said Cass. "I will make a snack for all of us."

"Can I help?" asked Sal.

"Oh, no thanks," said Alf. "Cass and Frits and I can handle it."

Sal felt as flat as the flat tire. He felt as if he were the laziest kid of all! He was the only one with no work to do. Even Golly was by the bus, acting as if it was his job to keep the Superkids safe.

9

Gus and Gert and Doc and Hot Rod came over.

"We can't finish fixing the flat," said Gert. "Now that the sun has set, we can't see. We will just have to hope for someone to stop and help us."

"We need a signal," said Sal. "I have just the thing."

Sal got on top of the bus. He waved his fluffy, shocking-pink monster doll. It was a perfect signal. It seemed to be floating in the black sky.

SCREECH! A big, red fire truck skidded to a stop next to the bus. Three firefighters got out. They said, "What a signal! We couldn't miss that pink monster! Do you need help?"

"Yes!" said Sal.

The fire truck lit up the bus. Gus and Gert finished fixing the tire.

The Superkids waved good-by to the firefighters. They said, "Thank you!"

"You are welcome!" said the firefighters. "Come visit us!"

"Sal, you should be the first one to visit," said Oswald. "You saved the day. And you did it all by yourself."

"No," said Sal. "I had help." He grinned and waved his shocking-pink monster doll.

"Do you want me to put your doll next to me when we get on the bus?" asked Cass.

"Oh, no thanks," said Sal. "I can handle it."